CW00864244

Kelvin Crab and the Message in a Bottle

Written and illustrated by Andy McGuinness

From the Whistle-On-Sea series

Copyright © 2019 Andy McGuinness

All rights reserved.

ISBN: 9781653314607

For Archie and Will

Come with me to Whistle-On-Sea…

It was a lovely sunny day at Whistle-on-Sea. Kelvin Crab was sitting outside Beach Hut Betty, busy writing a note.

He had just finished and was feeling very pleased with himself when his friends, Megan and Sam arrived with Bertie Bucket and Sandy Spade.

"Hello, Kelvin," said Bertie. "We've been having bucket loads of fun. Sam's been showing us how to build the most amazing sandcastles.

"You should have joined us," said Sandy. "You could have carved some shapes in the sand with your claws."

"I would have liked that," replied Kelvin. "But I've been busy writing a note to let everyone know about my rock concert at the Rock Pool tonight."

He held up the note for them all to read. "What do you think?" Everyone gathered round to read what Kelvin had written.

Megan noticed there were one or two spelling mistakes, but she didn't want to upset Kelvin by pointing them out. Kelvin did, after all, seem very pleased with what he'd written.

"You've done it very neatly," said Megan. "What are you going to do with it?"

"I'm going to put it in here," replied Kelvin holding up a bottle. "It's going to be a message in a bottle."

"Are you sure that's a good idea?" said Sam. "A message in a bottle is for when you've been shipwrecked at sea and washed up on a desert island. You throw the bottle out to sea hoping someone will find it and rescue you."

"You'd be better pinning it to the groynes like a poster," said Bertie. "Then lots of people walking up and down the beach will see it."

"No, this will work much better, you'll see," said Kelvin rolling up his letter and placing it in the bottle.

He carefully screwed on the cap, then excitedly scurried down to the sea to launch it.

"Oh dear," said Megan watching Kelvin place his bottle in the water. "I'm not sure people will see his message in a bottle.

We need to do something otherwise no one will turn up for the concert."

"We could make some signs for him," suggested Sandy.

"That's a great idea," replied Megan. "But it must remain a secret, we don't want to upset Kelvin. Come on, let's get to work gang."

And off they all went.

Bertie and Sandy headed straight for a clear patch of sand and wrote a message in big letters for everyone to see.

"Dig it!" yelled Sandy when they'd finished.

Shelby Seagull flew across the beach trailing a large banner from his beak.

And Sally Starfish gathered pebbles and shells and wrote a message on the seabed.

"I'm going to make Kelvin a super star, just like me," she said as she spelt out his name.

While the gang was busy making signs, Kelvin and his band were busy rehearsing down at the Rock Pool.

"Now we're rocking!" said Cozy Crab on the drums. He was getting very hot. And turning very red.

"You're looking a bit cooked there Cozy," said Kelvin. "How about we take a break?" he suggested.

Kelvin and the Crabettes clawed their way across the rocks and slid into the pool of cool seawater that had collected like a large lake.

As they cooled down, Kelvin couldn't help but wonder how many people had seen his message in a bottle. He felt very excited.

But had he known the truth, he wouldn't have been at all excited, because no one had seen his message.

The bottle was still bobbing about on the waves, drifting further and further out to sea.

Back on dry land, Megan and the gang continued to spread the news about the rock concert.

They painted a piece of driftwood and propped it up against the groynes.

"That should do the trick," said Megan. "Lots of people will know about Kelvin's concert."

"I hope so," said Sam. "If nobody turns up other than us, Kelvin will be terribly disappointed."

The hours passed and back at the Rock Pool, Kelvin and the band were ready to perform.

They had set up all their instruments and were waiting for everyone to arrive.

"This is going to be great," said Kelvin to his band mates. "I'm so excited."

The three crabs waited for their fans to arrive. They waited. And waited. But no one came.

"Where is everyone?" said Kelvin starting to feel sad.

"Perhaps no one saw your message in a bottle after all," said Cozy.

"You might be right," replied Kelvin. "I should have listened to Megan and Sam."

But then suddenly…

"We're here," cried a voice. Kelvin turned to see Megan, Sam, Bertie and Sandy coming down the beach. Suzy Starfish was also with them, and so were Seamus Seaweed and Willie Whelk.

Kelvin was pleased to see his friends, but he couldn't hide his disappointment that no one else was here.

"You were right, Megan, my message in a bottle didn't work," he said.

"Wait, look Kelvin," said Sam pointing to the water's edge.

Coming out of the sea were hundreds of crabs all chanting Kelvin's name. "Kelvin! Kelvin! Kelvin!"

"You got my message!" said Kelvin to the biggest of the crabs.

"Of course," said the crab, thinking he meant the message Suzy had left on the seabed, and not Kelvin's message in a bottle, which of course he hadn't seen at all.

"Brilliant!" said Kelvin with a smile.

Then he heard more voices. It was Marcel Moulé, Larry Lobster and Sandra Shrimp.

"We saw your message, Kelvin," said Larry, meaning the one Megan and Sam had painted on driftwood.

"So did we," It was Freddie Flotsam and Jessie Jetsam who had read Bertie and Sandy's message in the sand.

"Have we missed the concert?" said another voice.

Kelvin turned to see dozens of seagulls lined up along the groynes.

"You got my message too?" asked Kelvin.

"Loud and clear," said a seagull, thinking he meant the banner Shelby had flown across the sky.

Suddenly they heard a voice from out at sea.

"Yoo-hoo!"

It was Fisherwoman Florence in her boat, surrounded by fish leaping out of the water.

"We got your message," she yelled.

And this time she really had got Kelvin's message.

She was waving his message bottle in the air for them all to see. "It worked Megan!" said Kelvin." I knew it would."

"Well done," said Megan feeling pleased for Kelvin. She didn't want to upset him by mentioning the other messages.

All that mattered was that everyone was here for the concert.

"Come on Crabettes," said Kelvin grabbing his guitar. "We've got a rock concert to perform."

Kelvin stood on a rock.

"Thanks for coming, everyone. This is a very special song by a group called The Sea Police. It's called Message in a Bottle."

"Let's rock!" said the Crabettes.

Kelvin struck his guitar with his huge claw and everyone began to cheer.

The beach was alive with the sound of music and everyone dancing, including Florence, who bobbed to the music on her boat, waving her arms - and Kelvin's message in a bottle.

The End

More stories in the Whistle-On-Sea series

Bertie Bucket and Sandy Spade are collecting shells to paint on the beach. They find an Oyster Shell, which they hope will contain a pearl. But when an evil seagull called Bagshot kidnaps Bertie and the Oyster Shell, it's left to Shelby Seagull to save the day. Find out how in Bertie Bucket and the Precious Pearl.

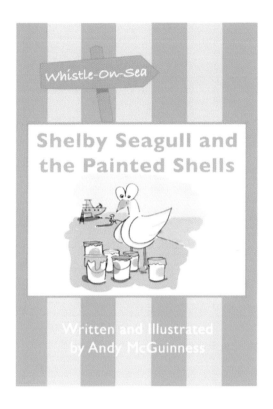

It's a day of painting shells for Megan and the gang, but when the paint runs dry, Shelby Seagull goes in search of fresh supplies. He returns with pots more paint for Larry Lobster and Willie Whelk to splodge and splat on bucket loads of shells. It's only later they discover that what Shelby found was no ordinary paint. Join the fun when Kelvin Crab discovers he has glow-in-the-dark paint on his claws in Shelby Seagull and The Painted Shells.

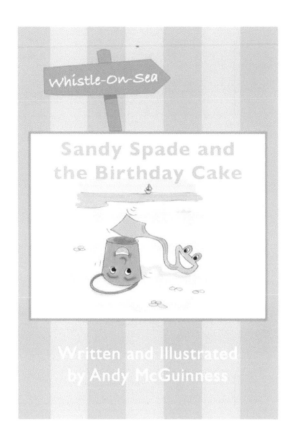

Sandy Spade and the Birthday Cake

Written and Illustrated by Andy McGuinness

It's Megan's birthday, but Bertie Bucket and Sandy Spade don't have the right ingredients to make her a birthday cake. To everyone's excitement, Sandy suggests they make it from sand and so the gang sets about making the best birthday cake ever. But when they come to present it to Megan, they can't believe their eyes - someone has started to eat it. Find out who in Sandy Spade and the Birthday Cake.

Follow us on Facebook

ABOUT THE AUTHOR

Andy McGuinness has spent his career as an advertising copywriter in London. Inspired by many happy summers spent in Whitstable with his two small boys, he has written the Whistle-On-Sea series.

Printed in Poland
by Amazon Fulfillment
Poland Sp. z o.o., Wrocław

53071611R00019